BLUE

Britta Teckentrup

ORCHARD

Blue lived in the deepest, darkest part of the forest. A place where sunlight never touched the ground.

Blue longed to feel the warmth of
the sun on his feathers, but he had long
forgotten how to fly. He perched on the
lowest branches of the Great Tree,
alone in the shadows.

The other birds didn't visit Blue anymore. Together they played above the treetops, never flying down to ask Blue if he would like to join in. "Blue's no fun anymore," they chirped.

"He just sits there all day. He never wants to play!"
Even Blue had forgotten what it felt like
to swoop and soar with his friends.

One evening, a new bird fluttered into the forest.
Wherever he flew, a little trail of golden light followed
him, and wherever he landed, green leaves
began to grow.

Yellow came to rest on the very
highest branch of the Great Tree.
Down below he saw Blue in the darkness.
"Hello!" he called gently. "I am Yellow."
But Blue didn't say anything.
He couldn't hear him.

Yellow watched over
Blue all through the night.
He hummed a soft tune.

The next morning,
Yellow

hopped

down

one

branch,

a little

closer to Blue.

Yellow's gentle humming
filled the forest. Blue wasn't
ready to talk yet, but
Yellow could wait. He had
all the time in the world.

On the first day,
Blue didn't
notice Yellow.

On the second day,
he could hear
a faraway tune.

On the third day,
he looked up,
ever so briefly.

And, day by day,
the world around Blue
began to change.

At last, Yellow landed
right next to Blue.
He reached out and
gently touched
Blue's wing.

Blue began to feel
warm inside.
And, for the first
time in a long while,
he opened his beak
and started to sing.

As the weeks passed, a new sound filled the forest: the gentle humming of two birds. The most beautiful song you could imagine. A song of hope, rising all the way up to the treetops.

Until the day
arrived when Blue
was ready to spread
his wings . . .

. . . and take to the skies.